IRON MAN

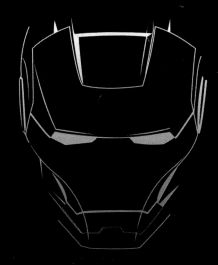

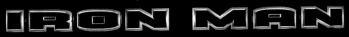

Iron Man: A New Hero
Printed in the United States of America.

For information address HarperCollins Children's Books, a division of HarperCollins Publishers,
1350 Avenue of the Americas, New York, NY 10019.
www.harpercollinschildrens.com
ISBN 978-0-06-082190-6
Book design by John Sazaklis
❖
First Edition

IRON MAN
A NEW HERO

ADAPTED BY **MARCO VALDO**
BASED ON THE SCREENPLAY BY **MARK FERGUS & HAWK OSTBY**
AND **ART MARCUM & MATT HOLLOWAY**
ILLUSTRATED BY **MARCELO MATERE**

HarperEntertainment
An Imprint of HarperCollins *Publishers*

A red-and-gold man made of iron flew through the sky and then used his thrusters to land safely. Though he looked like a robot, there was a man inside the iron suit; his name was Tony Stark.

Stark was a brilliant inventor and a billionaire. Stark wanted to build something to protect people. So he spent months creating an amazing suit that could fly, shoot laser blasts, and keep him safe inside. He wanted to be a hero.

Stark ran a company, Stark Industries, with the help of his assistant, Virginia Potts. He called her Pepper.

Stark Industries developed new technology for the military, and Stark often worked with his friend Lieutenant Colonel Jim Rhodes.

Only Pepper and the Lieutenant Colonel knew that Stark was the man inside the iron suit. They kept it a secret.

The suit was still a secret, too.

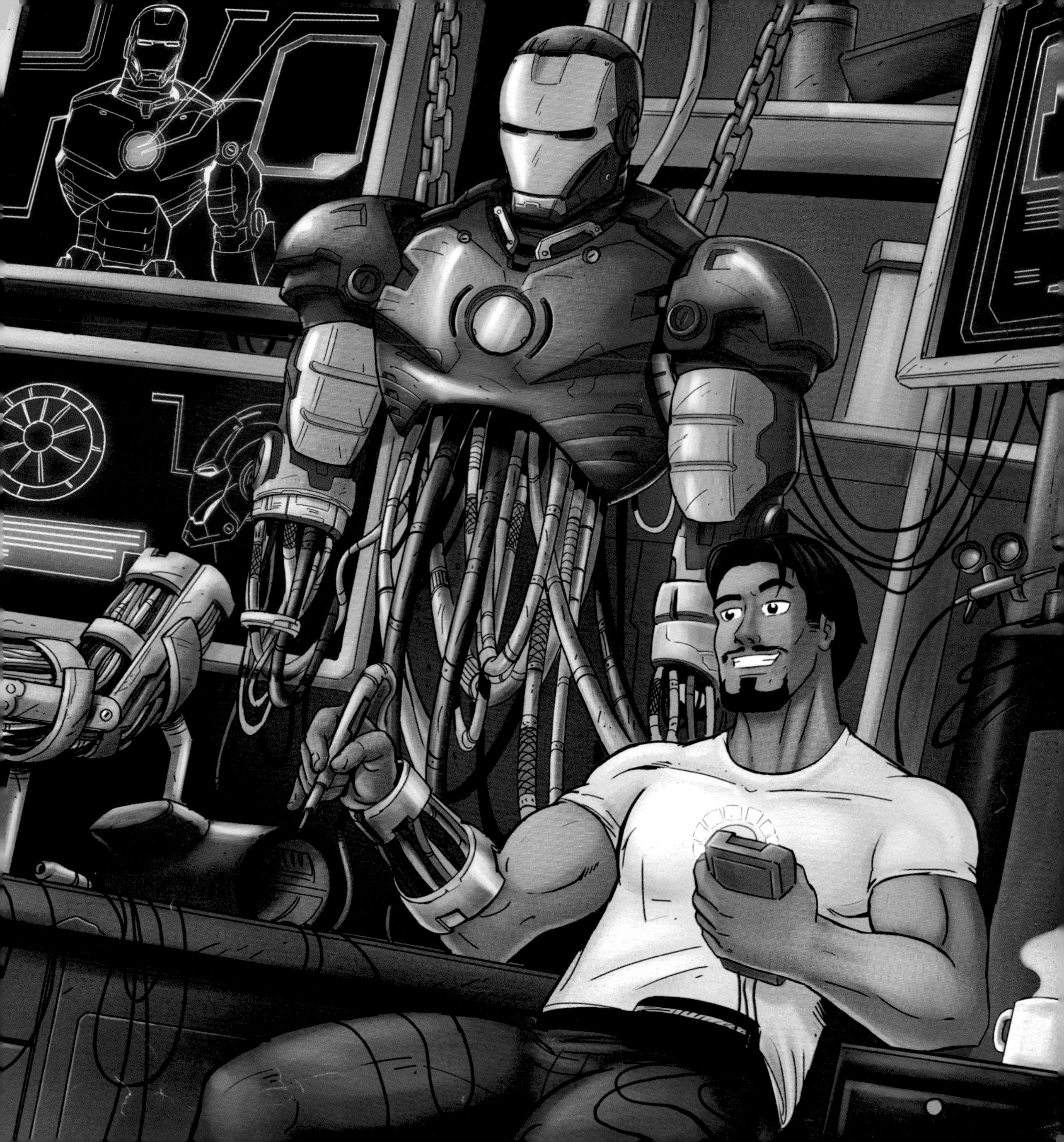

Stark flew the suit like a rocket out to the barren desert for tests. He wanted to make sure everything worked perfectly. No one could defeat this Iron Man . . . or so he thought!

Back at Stark Industries, Pepper made a shocking discovery. The designs for the iron suit had been stolen! Someone could use them to build another suit.

She sent a warning to Stark on the communication unit inside his suit. Then she heard a huge crash.

Pepper turned around and saw a giant gray iron man, but this wasn't Tony Stark. It was the villain who had stolen the suit designs. The gray giant's eyes glowed with blue lights.

Pepper stood in shock.
The giant smashed his fist into the ground. "I am Iron Monger!" he boomed.

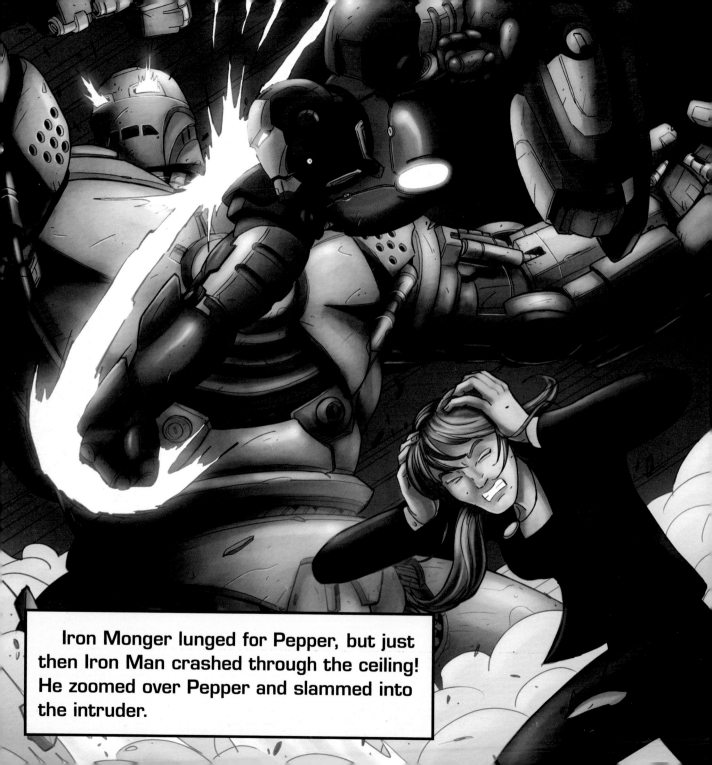

Iron Monger lunged for Pepper, but just then Iron Man crashed through the ceiling! He zoomed over Pepper and slammed into the intruder.

Iron Monger struggled back to his feet and shouted, "You've created the greatest weapon ever!"

This made Iron Man angry. He had designed his suit to help people, not hurt them.

The two metal giants rushed toward each other and crashed through the floor. Pipes broke and steam filled the room. Iron Man couldn't see through the steam.

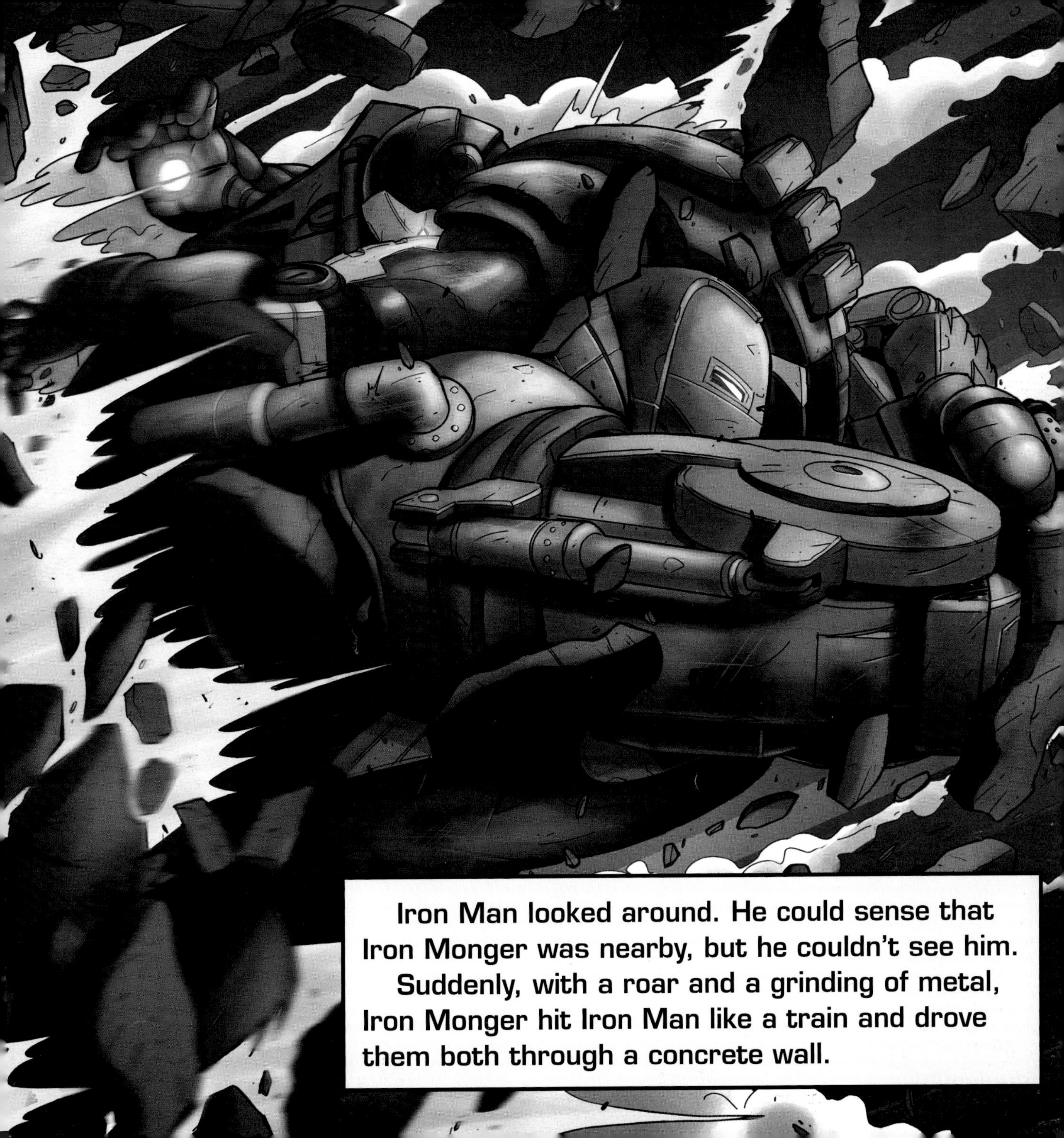

Iron Man looked around. He could sense that Iron Monger was nearby, but he couldn't see him.

Suddenly, with a roar and a grinding of metal, Iron Monger hit Iron Man like a train and drove them both through a concrete wall.

The battle spilled outside Stark Industries onto the highway. Cars and trucks came to a screeching halt as the two giants smashed onto the road.

Iron Monger grabbed a car, and prepared to throw it with his brute strength. Iron Man was quick to act—he blasted Iron Monger and knocked him to the ground.

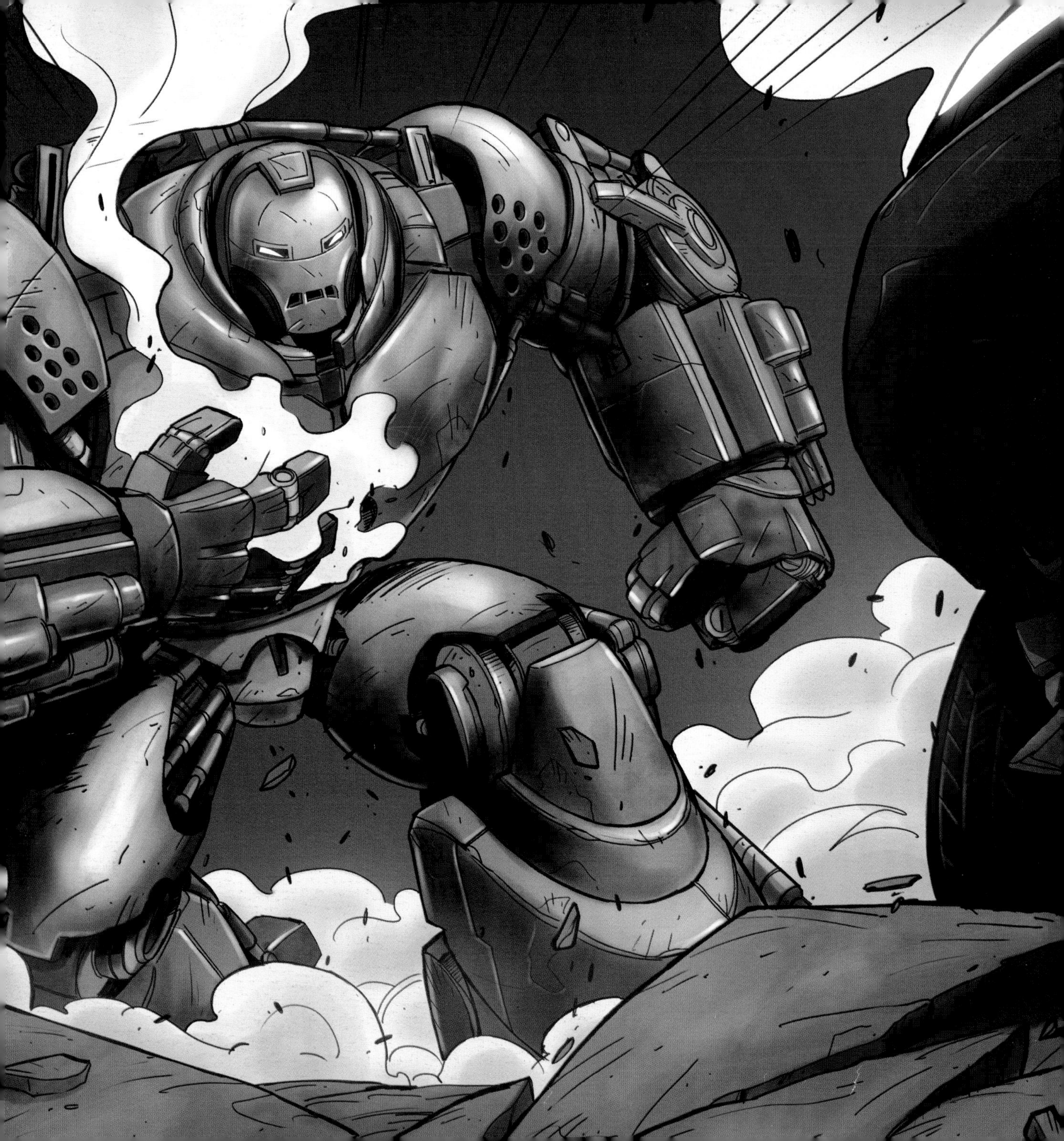

But the blast wasn't strong enough! Iron Monger rose again and hurled the car at Iron Man. It knocked the hero down, trapping him underneath.

Slowly, Iron Monger approached. Would this be the end of Iron Man?

As Iron Monger was about to deliver a crushing blow, Iron Man heard tires squealing. A large fuel truck was skidding, trying to stop, but it was no use.

The truck hit Iron Monger's leg, knocking him over. Iron Monger and the fuel truck burst into flames with a huge explosion.

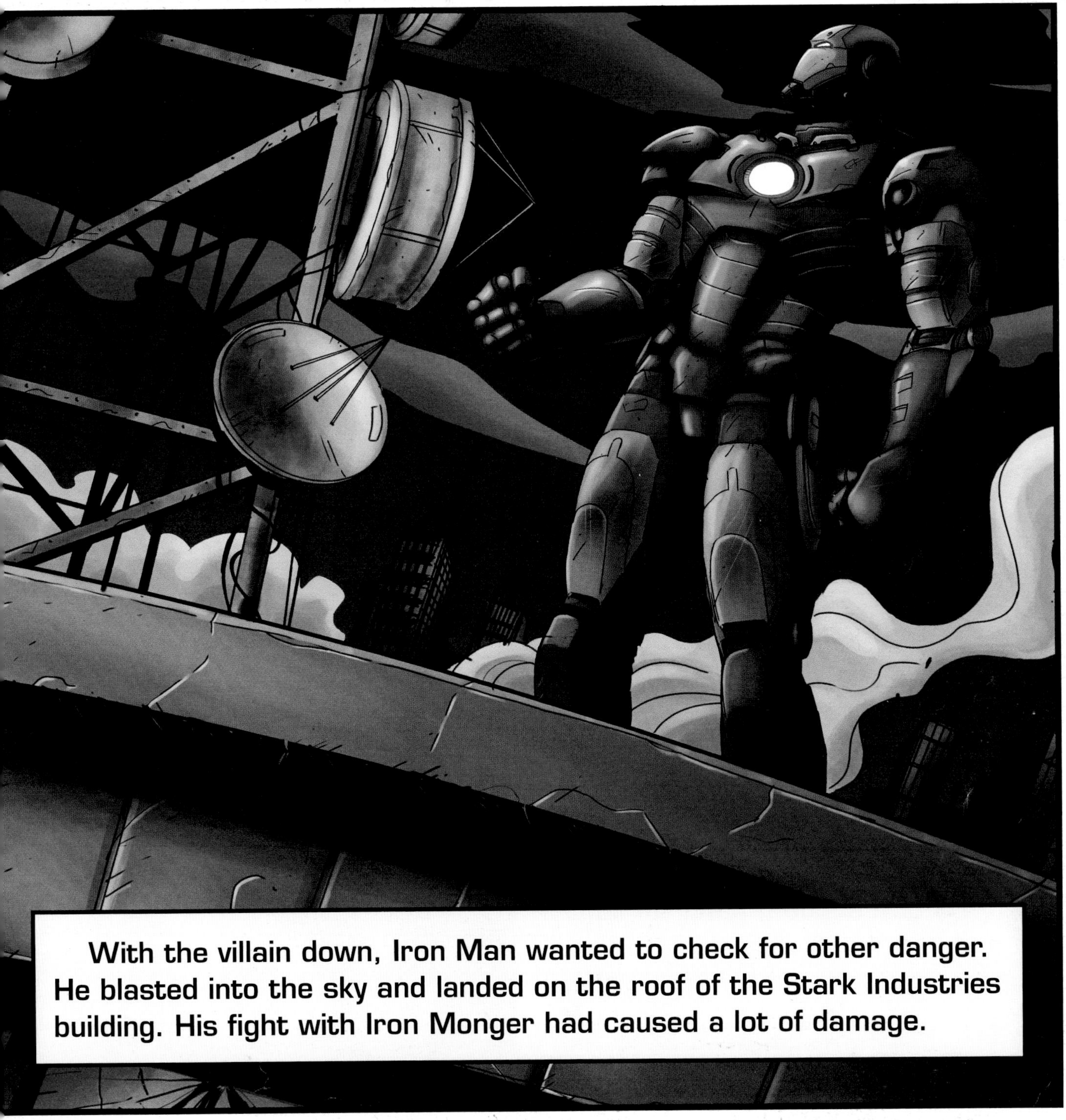

With the villain down, Iron Man wanted to check for other danger. He blasted into the sky and landed on the roof of the Stark Industries building. His fight with Iron Monger had caused a lot of damage.

All of a sudden, a blur of light and metal came crashing toward him—it was Iron Monger making one last attempt to destroy him!

Iron Man struggled with Iron Monger. Summoning all his power, Iron Man was able to blast the villain off of him.

The force of the gray giant's fall collapsed the roof, and the villain sank into the hole that opened up. He wasn't going to hurt anyone anymore.

Iron Man was still standing. His friends were safe.

The new hero knew that even though he won this fight, more battles were to come. He would be ready.